Dear Parent:
Your child's love of reading starts here!

Every child learns to read in a different way and at his or her own speed. Some go back and forth between reading levels and read favorite books again and again. Others read through each level in order. You can help your young reader improve and become more confident by encouraging his or her own interests and abilities. From books your child reads with you to the first books he or she reads alone, there are I Can Read Books for every stage of reading:

SHARED READING
Basic language, word repetition, and whimsical illustrations, ideal for sharing with your emergent reader

BEGINNING READING
Short sentences, familiar words, and simple concepts for children eager to read on their own

READING WITH HELP
Engaging stories, longer sentences, and language play for developing readers

READING ALONE
Complex plots, challenging vocabulary, and high-interest topics for the independent reader

ADVANCED READING
Short paragraphs, chapters, and exciting themes for the perfect bridge to chapter books

I Can Read Books have introduced children to the joy of reading since 1957. Featuring award-winning authors and illustrators and a fabulous cast of beloved characters, I Can Read Books set the standard for beginning readers.

A lifetime of discovery begins with the magical words "I Can Read!"

Visit www.icanread.com for information on enriching your child's reading experience.

In loving memory of Bing
—S.W.

To Carmen, with love
—J.M.

HarperCollins®, ☂®, and I Can Read Book® are trademarks of HarperCollins Publishers Inc.

Library of Congress Cataloging-in-Publication Data
Weeks, Sarah.
  Pip Squeak / by Sarah Weeks ; illustrated by Jane Manning.— 1st ed.
    p. cm. (An I can read book)
    Summary: Pip Squeak the mouse works hard to clean the house for his friend Max's visit, but then he has to clean up after Max too.
    ISBN-10: 0-06-075635-7 (trade bdg.) — ISBN-13: 978-0-06-075635-2 (trade bdg.)
    ISBN-10: 0-06-075637-3 (lib. bdg.) — ISBN-13: 978-0-06-075637-6 (lib. bdg.)
    [1. House cleaning—Fiction. 2. Friendship—Fiction. 3. Mice—Fiction. 4. Stories in rhyme.] I. Manning, Jane K., ill. II. Title.
III. Series.
PZ8.3.W4125Pip 2007   2005017873
[E]—dc22   CIP
                                                                   AC

1 2 3 4 5 6 7 8 9 10 ❖   First Edition

I Can Read!

BEGINNING 1 READING

Pip Squeak

by Sarah Weeks
Illustrated by Jane Manning

LAURA GERINGER BOOKS

An Imprint of HarperCollinsPublishers

Pip Squeak is a busy mouse.

Today he has to clean his house.

He has to get it done by three.

A friend is stopping by for tea.

Pip Squeak goes and gets a broom,
and sweep, sweep, sweep,
he sweeps the room.

He sweeps the steps.

He sweeps the floor.

He sweeps until his arms are sore.

Then Pip Squeak goes
and gets a mop,
and mop, mop, mop,
he does not stop.

8

He mops the steps.

He mops the floor.

And when he's done,

he mops some more.

Pip Squeak fluffs.

Pip Squeak flushes.

He gets the brush
and brush, brush, brushes.

Squirt! Squirt!

Rub! Rub!

Vroom! Vroom!

Scrub! Scrub!

Over.

Under.

Here and there.

Pip Squeak cleans up everywhere.

"Come in, Max. My house is neat.

Come in and visit. Have a seat."

But Max does not come have a seat,
and Max forgets to wipe his feet.

He throws his coat upon the floor.

And that's not all—

Max does much more.

He runs and jumps

on Pip Squeak's bed.

He puts a teacup

on his head.

Max is messy,

Max is icky.

Max makes everything feel sticky.

Over.

Under.

Here and there.

Max is messy everywhere!

Pip Squeak feels a little sad.

He also feels a little mad.

"My house was neat, Max.

Now it's not.

A messy house is what I've got."

"Oh, Pip," says Max,
"please don't feel bad.
I'll clean this mess—
then you'll be glad."

And so Max goes and gets the mop
and mop, mop, mop,
he does not stop.

He mops the floor, but that's not all.

He mops the windows and the wall.

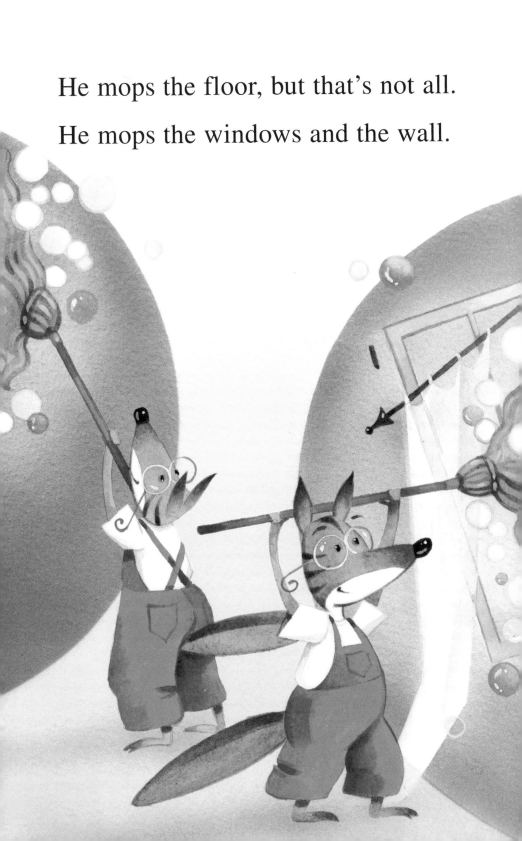

Clang! Bang!

Crash! Boom!

Mopping all around the room.

Over.

Under.

Left and right.

Max mops everything in sight.

"Good-bye," says Max,
and walks away.

28

"Wait!" cries Pip Squeak.

"Max, please stay.

Come back inside.

Come have some tea.

I'm glad you came to visit me.

I like you, Max, I really do.

But next time . . .

can I visit YOU?"